KINDNESS
SNIPPET JAR

Written & Illustrated
by Diane Alber

To my children, Ryan and Anna.
Always try to be kind, each and every day!

This kindness book belongs to:

_____

_____

_____

Just look at all those
amazing kindness notes!

I have to find my words! And quick...

This mosaic is for YOU!
The one reading this book!
I really hope you like it!

Sometimes all it takes
is doing something kind for someone
right in front of you!

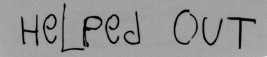

Snippet was so happy he finally made it into the kindness jar.

There are other snippets just like him
looking to make it into the jar, too! And you can help!

After YOU do a kind act, just write it down and
add it to a kindness snippet jar!
Encourage other kids to do the same to help
spread kindness everywhere!

Kindness Snippet Jar

There are two ways to use the Kindness Snippet Jar:

1) Every time you notice a child doing something kind, write it on a snippet and add it to the jar. Once the jar is full, everyone who contributed can receive a special reward.

2) Print kindness cards (available on www.dianealber.com) and place them in the jar. Have each child choose a card to prompt kindness throughout the day.

Made in the
USA
Middletown, DE